Sonny the Trick Horse

To Moggie

Chester Drawers

As a boy growing up on a hillside farm in southwest Missouri near Purdy, Eddie spent much of his time clearing new ground and raising strawberries. His parents taught him to be honest, work hard and treat people with respect. His interests include motivational speaking, inspirational teaching, and entertaining. For several years he has been a comedian on the Brumley music show in Branson, Missouri. He is also a song writer, musician and writer of inspirational and children's books.

Eddie and his wife, Evelyn, have four children and five grandchildren.

Eddie loves to tell stories of humor and common sense with practical applications for everyday life. He brings laughter and encouragement to readers and audiences of all ages.

Sonny the Trick Horse

By

Eddie Bowman

Illustrated by

Jane Lenoir

Bowman Publishing, Inc.
154 Whispering Oaks Drive
Galena, MO 65656
1-888-336-5132 or (417) 272-8839

Library of Congress cataloging-in-publication data

Bowman, Eddie, 1939-
Sonny the trick horse / by Eddie Bowman ; illustrated by Jane Lenoir.
p. cm.
Summary: Because he lacks self-confidence, Sonny uses tricks to resist learning what every horse needs to know, but finally he finds a way to put even his trickery to good use.
ISBN 1-931281-28-9 (cloth).
-- ISBN 1-931281-29-7 (pbk.)
[1. Horses--Fiction. 2. Tricks--Fiction. 3. Self-confidence--Fiction.]
I. Lenoir, Jane, 1950- ill. II. Title.
PZ7.B68345So 1998
[Fic]--dc21

96-540-11
CIP
AC

Printed in the United States of America

Contents

Dedicated to

my grandson Braden Clark Bowman

Chapter 1

Sonny Learns to Stand

Sonny was born one spring morning when the grass was beginning to grow. His mother said, "Get up, Sonny! You've got to learn to stand."

"But, Mother," he said, "I've never stood before."

"That doesn't matter," she replied. "There are lots of things you must learn to do. So get up. I know you can."

Sonny tried to get up, but he fell back down. Maybe if I act like I'm

sick, he thought, Mother won't make me get up. So he began to moan like he had a bellyache.

"Sonny," his mother asked, "is this some kind of a trick? I know you're not sick." She gave a neigh and Sonny's father came running.

He said, "Sonny, don't try to trick us. I know it's hard to get up, but set your mind to it. When I count to three, I want you to jump up. OK, here we go!" He pawed the ground three times.

Sonny tried as hard as he could to get up.

"You can do it! Come on, now!" said his father. Then with a groan, Sonny finally stood up! His parents were very proud of him.

"There, Sonny," his mother said, "we knew you could do it! And from now on, we don't want any more of this trick stuff. If you go around making excuses all the time, acting like you're sick when you're not, you're going to miss out on the good things of life. Now, tomorrow, you're going to learn to walk."

"OK," Sonny said.

Chapter 2

A Sick Trick

When Sonny awoke the next morning, the first thing he thought about was walking!

"This is the big day!" his mother said. "Get up and walk."

Sonny gave a heave, but as he was rising, a terrible pain hit him! Oh, no! he thought. If I tell her I'm sick, she'll think I'm trying to trick her again. So, he tried to ignore the pain. He stood up, but fell back down!

His mother laughed and said,

"Come on, boy, you can do better than that!"

Sonny struggled to get up again. Then everything started whirling around. He felt dizzy, then he passed out!

When he came to, his mother was calling, "Sonny, Sonny! Are you all right?"

"I feel better, now," he said.

"Why didn't you tell me you were sick, Sonny?" his mother asked.

"Well, I didn't want you to think I was doing that trick stuff," he replied.

She said, "Sonny, don't ever be afraid to tell me how you feel."

"OK," said Sonny.

In a short while, his bellyache was gone. He said, “Mother, I’m ready now. How do I walk?”

So she showed him how to walk. “That’s good, Sonny!” she said. “Now, tomorrow, you’re going to learn to trot!”

Chapter 3

Struck by a Duck!

Sonny didn't know about this trotting business. He told his parents that he would like to walk one more day before trying it, if they didn't mind.

"Oh, we don't mind at all," his mother said. "We don't want to push you before you're ready. But it is important that you learn to trot."

"Why is trotting so important?" Sonny asked.

"Well, for one thing," his father answered, "trotting is faster than walking. If you can't trot, you might be late when you need to be somewhere."

"Oh, I see," said Sonny. So Sonny spent one more day just walking. He felt like he needed this time to build up his confidence before he started something else. And he still wasn't sure he wanted to learn to trot.

His mother decided to go along with him for a while and let him learn a lesson by experience. "Sonny," she said, "let's go walking."

They walked for a long time and then stopped under the old apple tree. Sonny said, "I'm thirsty."

His mother said, "Well, go down to the pond and get a drink. I'll wait here for you."

Sonny walked to the pond and stuck his lips into the cool water. But as he was leaving, he accidentally stepped on the toe of a newly hatched

duckling. The duckling gave a squawk! Sonny heard a commotion and saw the duckling's mother running at him! She was really mad! Sonny thought, I've got to get out of here fast! So he started walking, but the angry duck followed him! He walked as fast as he could, but the duck gained on him!

"Oh, no!" he said. About that time he felt her flogging at his hocks!

"Oh, I wish I could trot!" he said.

Then his mother came and scared the duck away. "What's wrong, Sonny?" she asked.

"Oh, Mother," he said, "I couldn't get away from that mean old duck!

Mother, I think I need to learn how to trot!"

"That's a good idea, Sonny!" she said. "Tomorrow, we'll start teaching you."

"OK!" Sonny said.

Chapter 4

Sonny Learns to Trot

Sonny had sore hocks the next morning, but that just reminded him of the need to learn to trot. So after breakfast, he told his parents, "I'm ready. Now, how do you trot?"

His father went through the steps for him. "Now you try it," he said.

But Sonny got all mixed up. He put both front feet forward, then both hind feet forward. He looked like a big bullfrog hopping across the field!

"Whoa, Sonny!" his father called. "Now let's go back and start this over

again. You're a horse, not a frog!"

So they went over the steps very carefully. Before long, Sonny was trotting as pretty as you please! He said, "Mother, let's trot down to the old apple tree. Now, you stay here. I'm going to the pond. I'll call if I need you."

Just as he figured, the duck started chasing him, but Sonny went into a fast trot . . . then faster and faster as he left the duck behind!

"Atta boy, Sonny," his mother called.

"Boy," Sonny said, "I sure am glad I learned to trot!"

"Me, too," his mother replied. "And tomorrow, you're going to learn to run!"

and tied him up in a dark room! Then Harris showed up. He told the officials that Mr. Marion had had an emergency and had told him to ride Sonny. So they told Harris to get ready, for he was to perform in thirty minutes! Harris intended to make Sonny look so bad that his career would be over!

Sonny did some quick thinking. Harris rode Sonny to the middle of the arena and said, "Sonny wants to show you some of his tricks. First, he wants to tell you how old he is."

Sonny pawed, One, two, three, four, five, six . . . !

Harris tried to make him stop, but he kept right on! Sonny finally

stopped at thirty-nine! The arena roared with applause and laughter! Then Sonny lay down and played sick! Again the crowd cheered! Then Harris announced, "Now Sonny is going to kiss me." Sonny thought, That's what you think, you old buzzard! Instead, he got a mouthful of dirt, turned to Harris, and spit it all over him! Then he reached in Harris's back pocket, got his handkerchief, and gave it to him to clean himself

up! The audience died laughing! When Harris got on Sonny's back, Sonny started the bullfrog leap! It was hilarious! Then he gave a mighty buck and sent Harris straight up in the air!

About that time, Mr. Marion, who had managed to free himself, ran out to Sonny. They went around the arena in a breathtaking performance!

An old man in the crowd said, "I

remember a horse that showed here years ago. This Sonny reminds me somewhat of him. I think his name was Blick or Blis or something like that." Somebody else said, "Buck!"

"Yeah, that was it!" the old man said. "Buck! Boy, he was a dandy!"

Sonny had never felt so good! He was single-footing in the same arena as his grandfather! Then he went to the center of the ring and bowed! He and Mr. Marion won the highest honors!

When Sonny got back home, he told his parents all about the show! His mother said, "Sonny, we're so proud of you, and we know your grandpa would be, too!"

Sonny said, "Well, I'm lucky to have parents who love and encourage me like you always do. And you know what? I'm sure glad I learned that trick stuff!"

They talked into the night, then Sonny's father said, "Well, we'd better get some sleep. We have a busy day tomorrow."

"What's happening tomorrow?" Sonny asked.

"Oh, we didn't tell you," his father said. "You know that mean old duck? Well, she wants her kids to enter some kind of duck show at the fair. She has this stupid idea that you can teach them to leap like a frog and single-foot, so I told her you would

Chapter 6

Sonny Learns about Gaits

"Sonny, do you know what a gait is?" his mother asked.

"I sure do," Sonny answered. "There's one by the barn that Mr. Marion opens when he brings us hay."

"No!" his mother said. "That is spelled g-a-t-e, this is g-a-i-t! All horses have what is known as three natural gaits called walking, trotting, and galloping."

"You mean like me?" he asked.

"Yes, like you," she replied.

"But, Sonny, there are other gaits horses can learn. You might call them unnatural or artificial. But horses who learn them often get to travel to big horse shows and perform before thousands of people!"

"When can I learn these gaits?" Sonny asked.

"Well," she said, "I heard Mr. Marion talking yesterday. He really likes you. He thinks you have great ability, and he wants to train you!"

"Please, tell me more about these other gaits," Sonny said. "What are they like?"

"Oh, they are beautiful!" replied his mother. "One is called a rack, or single-foot. Your grandfather Buck went to the national horse show in New York City one year and won honors with this gait!"

"Man!" Sonny said. "Wouldn't that be great if I could go to New York City where Grandpa went!"

"Well, you never know, Sonny," said his mother. "You never know!"

Chapter 7

Sonny Learns Tricks

Mr. Marion and Sonny got along just fine. But then something happened that Sonny did not like! Mr. Marion said, "Sonny, I want to teach you some tricks. Yes, Sonny, I want you to lie down and start groaning like you have a bellyache."

But Sonny just stood there.

"Well, maybe tomorrow," said Mr. Marion.

Sonny went back to the barnyard with his head low. His father said, "Sonny, why the long face?"

Sonny said, “Mr. Marion is trying to get me to do that trick stuff you told me was wrong!”

“What kind of tricks?” his father asked.

“Oh, he wants me to act like I’m sick when I’m really not!” Sonny answered.

“Sonny,” his mother said, “he wants you to do cute stuff. People call it tricks. There’s nothing wrong with that. But that does not mean that you are dishonest or trying to fool somebody. Actually, we would be proud to have another trick horse in the family!”

“Another trick horse?” Sonny asked.

"Yes, your grandfather Buck," she replied. "You should have seen him in New York City! After his performance, he bowed for everyone."

"Wow!" Sonny said, "maybe I could learn to do that!"

The next morning, Mr. Marion found Sonny eager to learn. He taught Sonny to play sick, count with his feet, bow, shake his head *no* or nod *yes*, and swipe Mr. Marion's handkerchief! Sonny even learned to kiss Mr. Marion! He worked hard to use his talents and to develop into a fine show horse! Mr. Marion said, "Sonny, I think you're ready to go places! What do you say?"

Sonny nudged him a little bit with his nose and nodded his head up and down. "Well, I'll be!" said Mr. Marion. "I think we've got a real winner!"

Chapter 8

The Big Show

For the next few months, Mr. Marion and Sonny went to horse shows and rodeos. People raved about their performances! Then an invitation came from New York City. "Dear Mr. Marion, We would be pleased to have you and Sonny perform at this year's horse show."

Everybody was thrilled about it! Everybody, that is, except a man named Harris and his horse, Hobo! Harris was jealous because he had not received an invitation, so he began thinking up an evil plan! When Sonny and Mr. Marion arrived in New York City, Sonny was given a nice, clean stall. As the time

approached for the show to begin, someone told Mr. Marion that he had a phone call. As he walked down a long hallway, two men grabbed him